PEM PEM'S BIRTHDAY

Peter Bently
Duncan Beedie

Hello! This is a story about four friendly monsters who live on Planet Pok.

This is **Nid**.

This is **Gop**.

This is **San**.

This is **Pem Pem**.

They have a funny way of talking. It's called Monsters' Nonsense.

See if you can read what they are saying. Ready?

Pem Pem was excited.
It was his birthday.
He was going to fly
all his friends in his
spaceship for a special
birthday picnic.

Rup teg teg

The monsters started to gather tasty treats for the picnic. Except for Nid, who was still fast asleep.

San zipped to the Blue Broccoli Bush to pick some blue broccoli.

And Gop nipped to the Fizzy Fountain to fetch a flask of lemonade.

Pem Pem made his favorite dessert. But it kept jumping off the plate!

Gip dup cad!

Pem Pem quickly stuffed the jello into his special jumping jello box.

Then he went outside to look for his spaceship. But where was it? He was sure he'd parked it outside his cave.

San hadn't seen the spaceship.

Rog?

Gop hadn't seen it either.

Tem?

The three monsters decided to go and look for it together.

Uck uck

The monsters looked behind the Tentacle Tree.

Then they searched by the Emerald Rocks. But, it wasn't there either.

Pem Pem scratched both his heads. Where on Planet Pok could his spaceship be?

Suddenly the monsters heard a noise.

Pid pid teck!

BOING! BOING! BOING!

Oh no!
The jumping jello had escaped!

The monsters chased the jello all the way back to Pem Pem's cave. It was bouncing all over the place.

Dit dit

Then... Ker-BOING! Pog

Nid sat up and yawned. He was very sorry about the jello. But wait! What was that?

Gup gan

Oh dear. It was Pem Pem's spaceship.

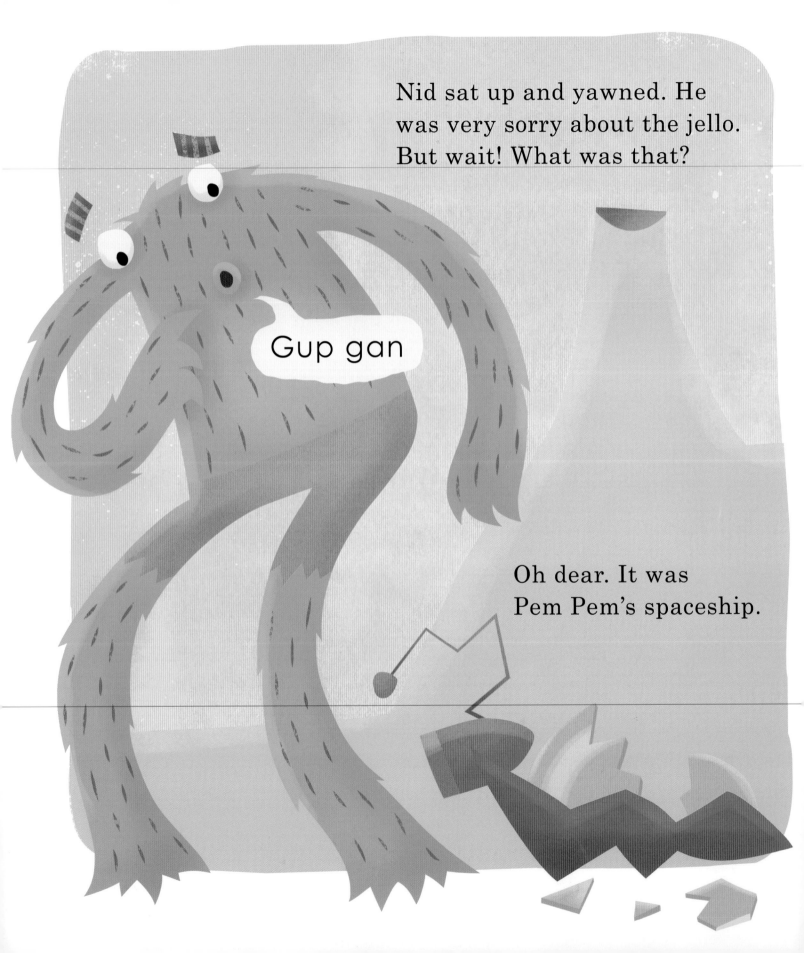

Pem Pem shook his heads sadly at the squashed spaceship. He had no jumping jello and no spaceship. He wasn't having a very good birthday at all!

Pem Pem was sad and went into his cave.

How could the monsters cheer him up?

Dap dat

San had an idea!

San flew to the Glass Bubble Gulch. She spotted a big orange bubble. Perfect!

Then Gop found a couple of old engines in her crater.

Nid helped San and Gop attach the engines to the orange glass bubble.

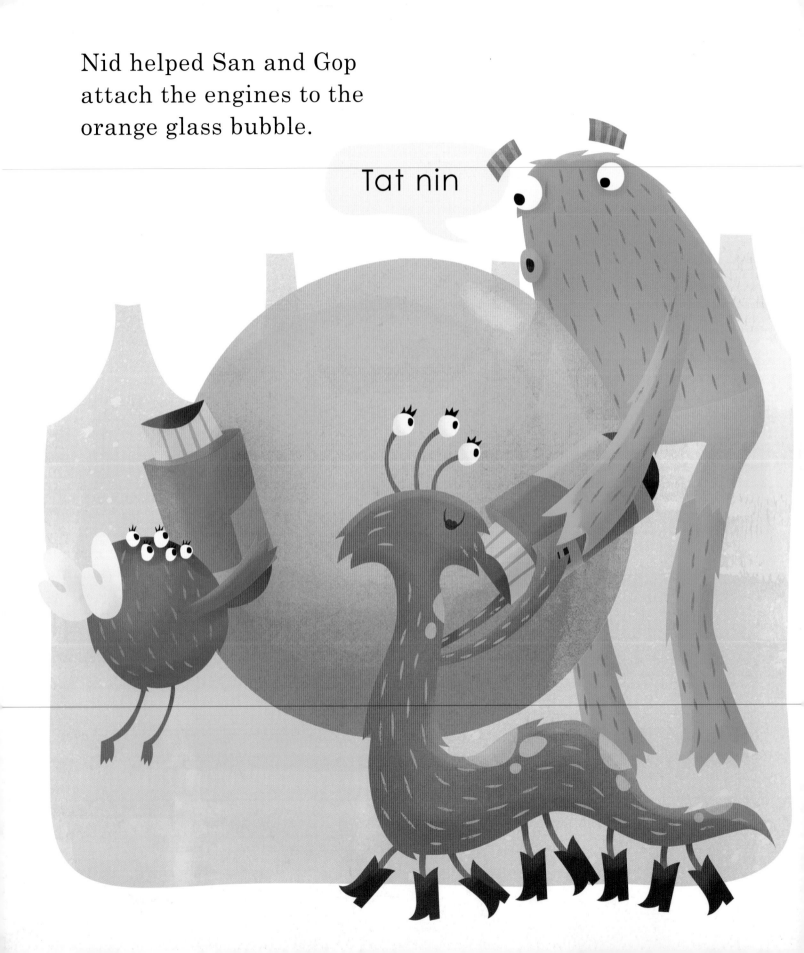

Ta-da! San, Gop, and Nid had made Pem Pem a new spaceship.

Rad

Meck nem nem!

Pem Pem was delighted. Now they could fly away for a birthday picnic after all.

The monsters climbed
aboard the spaceship.

But where was Nid?
Hurry up, slowpoke!

At last the monsters flew into the sky. **Whoosh!**

The spaceship started to wobble all
over the place. What was the matter?

Pem Pem quickly landed
on top of Hairy Hill.
What a bumpy ride!

Nid had a special surprise
for Pem Pem. It was a
new jumping jello.

The monsters laughed. No wonder the spaceship had been so wobbly!

Happy Birthday, Pem Pem.

Reading with your monsters!

Monsters' Nonsense is all about having fun while learning the skills of reading. If children have fun reading, they'll want to do it more.

What helps children with their reading?

Phonics: the ability to sound out (decode) words that they don't know.

Reading comprehension: to read for meaning so that they can understand and enjoy the story.

The *Monsters' Nonsense* series is designed to support these skills to help children become successful, happy readers and to encourage a positive, shared reading experience.

The adult reader (or reading mentor) reads the main narrative—supporting reading comprehension and bringing the story alive.

The child reads the Monsters' Nonsense in the speech bubbles. These are "non-words" to help them practice their decoding skills at a level that is right for them. It's important that your child knows that these "non-words"are not real words and have no meaning.

More monster fun

Monster Questions Ask your child questions about the story. For example, who is their favorite monster? Why did Pem Pem have to lock the jello in a box? Where did the monsters look for the spaceship? What did San use to make the new spaceship? What made the new spaceship wobble? Do they think that Pem Pem had a good birthday?

I SPY Play "I spy with my little eye" using the phonemes in the book. For example, "I spy with my little eye something beginning with the phonemes /j/ and /j/." Answer: "jumping jello." You can take turns. Remember, be sure to use sounds and not letter names for this activity.

Make More Monsters Encourage your child to draw or make some more monsters for Planet Pok. Make up some new names and see if your child can spell them.

Rhyming Nonsense Encourage your child to generate real and non-words that rhyme with the monster names. For example, Nid, Sid, did, mid, and so on.

Create a Monster Play Work with your child to create a Monster Play. Think of a plot and act out the story together, using real and non-words.

Phonics glossary

blend to blend individual sounds together to pronounce a word, e.g. s-n-a-p blended together reads snap.

digraph two letters representing one sound, e.g. sh, ch, th, ph.

grapheme a letter or a group of letters representing one sound, e.g. t, b, sh, ch, igh, ough (as in "though").

High Frequency Words (HFW) are words that appear most often in printed materials. They may not be decodable using phonics (or too advanced) but they are useful to learn separately by sight to develop fluency in reading.

phoneme a single identifiable sound, e.g. the letter "t" represents just one sound and the letters "sh" represent just one sound.

segment to split up a word into its individual phonemes in order to spell it, e.g. the word "cat" has three phonemes: /c/, /a/, /t/.

vowel digraph two vowels which, together make one sound e.g. ai, oo, ow.

Remember to praise your child and enjoy the shared reading experience.

Quarto is the authority on a wide range of topics.

Quarto educates, entertains and enriches the lives of our readers—enthusiasts and lovers of hands-on living.

www.quartoknows.com

Publisher: Maxime Boucknooghe
Editorial Director: Victoria Garrard
Art Director: Miranda Snow
Editor: Sophie Hallam
Designer: Mike Henson
Consultant: Carolyn Clarke

Copyright © QEB Publishing, Inc 2016

First published in the United States in 2016 by QEB Publishing, Inc.
Part of The Quarto Group
6 Orchard
Lake Forest, CA 92630

A CIP record for this book is available from the Library of Congress.

ISBN 978 1 60992 911 4

Printed in China

4043